ANOTHER MONSTER AT THE END OF THIS BOOK

Written by Jon Stone
Illustrated by Michael Smollin

A GOLDEN BOOK · NEW YORK

randomhousekids.com   SesameStreetBooks.com   www.sesamestreet.org
Educators and librarians, for a variety of teaching tools, visit us at RHTeachersLibrarians.com
ISBN 978-0-375-97651-3
This special edition was printed for Kohl's Department Stores, Inc. (for distribution on behalf of Kohl's Cares, LLC, its wholly owned subsidiary) by Random House Children's Books, a division of Penguin Random House LLC, New York.

KOHL'S
Style: 97651
Factory Number: 126509
Production Date: 05/2017

MANUFACTURED IN CHINA
10 9 8 7 6 5 4 3 2 1

ENOUGH is ENOUGH!

I, Grover, am now GLUING this page down so you CANNOT turn it.

And if you cannot turn the page we will not get to The MONSTER that is at The End of This Book!

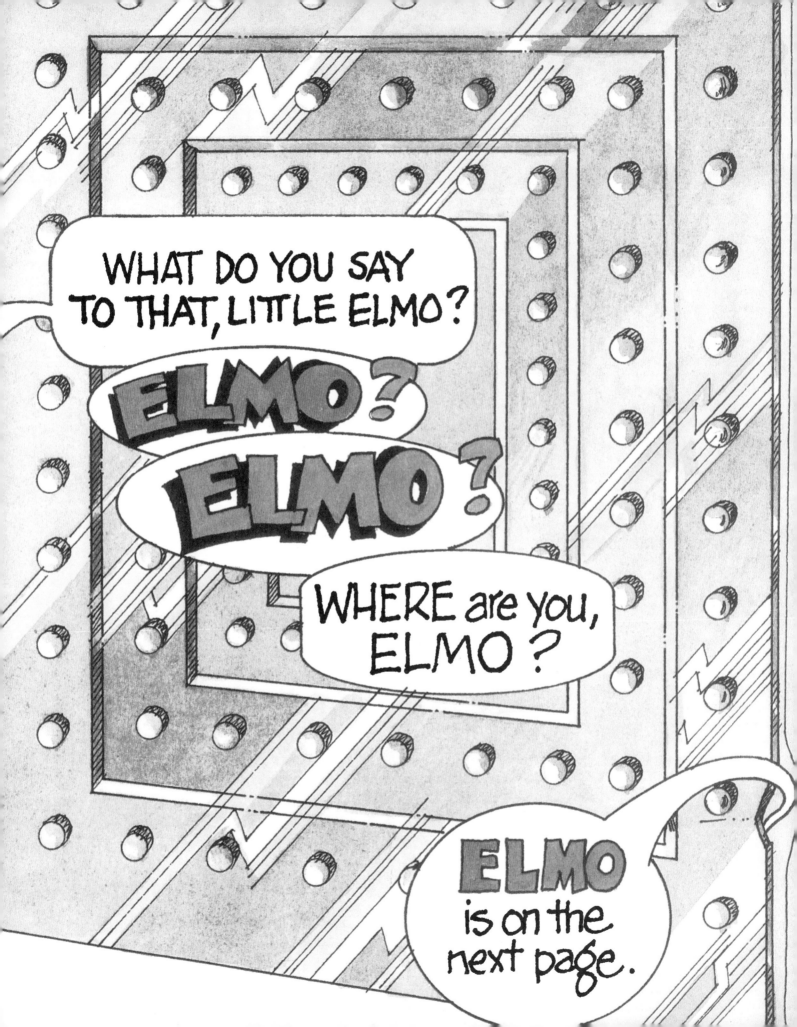